My dear Aunt Moonbeam,

Ever since I found out everyone in Weavewillow is as excited about dragons as I am, I've been thinking of ways to learn more about those amazing creatures so that I can send the knowledge back home. Even with all I've written about dragons and their kind, there is so much more to discover! The gold dragon I rode and adventured with while writing A Practical Guide to Dragon Riding had a great idea—he thought there was no better way to learn about dragons than to go live among them.

I set off at once for red dragon territory. I had many adventures under the wings of the dragons who took me in and taught me about their magic, their secrets, and their ways. One day, my dragon friends assure me, I will be able to do dragon magic as well—but first I have a choice to make. I can either study magic under a master dragon wizard, or I can take a dragon as an apprentice myself and learn from it just as it learns from me! What a tough choice—I want to do both!

This new book contains everything I've learned about the mysteries of dragonkind. Perhaps you can read it around the hearth at home to the cousins so that everyone can help me decide which path I should take next. Please write back.

Dragons forever!

Sindri

Written inside the Library of Palanthas, 357AC

A Practical Guide to
Dragon Magic

Inscribed by

Sindri Suncatcher

The Greatest Kender Wizard
Who Ever Lived
(and Honorary Dragon!)

DEALING WITH DRAGON MAGIC

Dragons have magic running through their veins. This natural connection with magic combined with their incredibly long life span has led dragons to become some of the world's most powerful spellcasters.

Dragon magic is elemental magic, meaning dragons can harness the elements to power their spells. Common elements are fire, lightning, ice, poison, and acid. The element a dragon channels is determined by its heritage, but the form the dragon's magic takes reflects the personality and the education of the individual dragon.

You can tell based on the color of the dragon's scales!

A dragon's breath weapon is the simplest expression of its magical power. Even in the egg, dragons can use this most basic form of magic. Hatchlings cough forth elemental magic to help them break open their shell. However, just because they are natural magic-users doesn't mean they don't need help in learning how to harness the power. The more complex the spell, the more studying a dragon has to do to be able to cast it.

This first breath of magic is called the irthrae.

DRAGON ETIQUETTE

Remember, even a baby dragon is likely to see you as an amusing animal at best, and a tasty snack at worst! That is why it is important to be very polite at all times.

1. Bring a gift when approaching a dragon for the first time and at least once a month thereafter.

2. Be polite at all times–always say "please" and "thank you."

3. Bow when entering or leaving a dragon's presence.

4. Speak in formal Draconic.

5. Work hard!

6. Don't talk down to a dragon.

7. Don't use items made from dragons. *Unless they were gifts*

8. Never steal from a dragon.

9. Don't run away from a dragon. *This engages their predatory instincts!*

10. Never lie to a dragon. *They can always, always tell!*

Magic to the Core

Even those who are uneducated in the ways of dragons can take advantage of dragon magic by using parts of a dragon's body in their spells. The bones and blood of dragons hold magic—magic that can be used by wizards to make their spells more potent and to craft amazing magical items. The magic is always most potent if donated willingly by a living dragon, but convincing a dragon to part with a piece of eggshell or a shed scale can be as difficult as fighting the dragon tooth and claw! Anyone who possesses a piece of a dragon can use it to curse the dragon it belongs to, sometimes even compelling that dragon's eternal obedience, and few dragons are willing to risk their health and freedom to give a wizard a spell component, no matter how kind or persuasive the wizard.

Most dragon-enhanced items are either made by dragons or their human apprentices, who are bound never to use the draconic items against their master. A few are made from the remains of dead dragons—evil dragons slain by valiant heroes, or good dragons passing away from old age. But using dragon remains is frowned upon in civilized society, and those butchers who would desecrate a dragon's corpse often become victims of draconic justice.

Unfortunately, expensive and complex rituals are required to keep draconic components from rotting or turning to dust within a month—and even more rituals are required if you want to retain some of their innate elemental powers.

Eggshell: Powdered dragon eggshells have powerful healing and elemental resistance properties if mixed properly into the right potion.

Scales: Stronger than steel but flexible, dragonscale armor is much sought after. Dragonscale boots enable you to walk across lava!

Teeth: Sharp and durable, dragon teeth make excellent swords, arrowheads, daggers, and other weapons. Dragons shed their teeth multiple times as they grow bigger, making teeth among the easiest draconic components to come by.

Claws: Dragon claw clippings, when stewed and enchanted properly, make excellent sharpening ointments.

Horns: Hollowed out and fitted with a cap, a dragon horn can hold acidic agents so potent they would eat through glass or crystal. Dragon horns are one of the few containers that can store dragon blood.

Blood: Dragon blood hisses and bubbles with magic and can be contained only in a specially enchanted vial. When used instead of ink in a wizard's spell, it makes the spell almost foolproof.

Spit: Depending on the type of dragon, dragon spit has a variety of magical properties that always link up with the dragon's type of elemental magic.

Organs: Organs also possess magical powers, but only a dark wizard would ever use them!

Dragon Spellcraft

Dragon magic takes four basic forms: combative, defensive, controlling, and communicative. Most humans are familiar with a dragon's combative magic, but did you know it can also use its magic to control the weather, talk to animals, or create icy armor?

Combative Magic

The flashiest magic in a dragon's repertoire is a dragon's combative spells. The most basic form of combative magic is the breath weapon, but dragons can also use their magic to cause the earth to tremble, to summon venomous insects, to drain the strength from their victims, and to blind their foes.

Who wouldn't want to breathe fire?

And the hoard within

Defensive Magic

Dragons dislike being injured just as much as humans do. Luckily, dragons can use elemental magic to protect themselves and their lairs. Dragons can raise up walls of stone or ice, summon fog or darkness to cloud their territory, and create a moat of sucking mud. Dragons also use their magic to protect the only thing they care about more than their treasure—their own skin. Dragons have been seen to create icy armor, put their victims to sleep, and freeze their foes in place with a glare.

Talk about a cold stare!

Controlling Magic

When you have an ego as big as a dragon's and the power to match, you get very good at using your magic to convince everything—plants, humans, the elements, hidden treasures, gravity, the weather—to do as you command. *I'll make it perfectly sunny every day!*

Communicative Magic

Chromatic dragons tend to communicate with their bellies. But metallic dragons are often as curious about us as we are about them! These dragons have learned how to use magic to send their voices far away, to talk to animals or plants, and to read your thoughts.

Ooh! I want to be able to read thoughts!

> ## DRAGON SPIRITS
>
> When a dragon's body dies, its spirit often lingers as an expression of the dragon's magical essence. This spirit retains the personality of the dragon, helping or hindering passersby in accordance with the beliefs the dragon held in life.

As in, "Rawr! I'd like you better in my belly!"

Talking with Dragons

If you are interested in dragons, you'll want to learn a bit of their language and the proper etiquette for dealing with dragons. While most dragons speak Common, speaking to a dragon in its own language encourages a dragon to stop thinking about you in terms of food. In addition, many of their spells and books about magic are written in Draconic. Legend has it that dragon writing is highly magical and is necessary for a dragon's most powerful spells.

Commonly the size of a cart, and about as heavy as one too!

Draconic Script

IMPORTANT DRACONIC WORDS AND PHRASES

Here are some words and phases you'll definitely want to memorize before you search out any dragons or adopt a dragon familiar.

TERMS OF ADDRESS IN DRACONIC

Leader (teacher): *maekrix*

Pet (human apprentice): *kosjirl*

Friend (dragon companion): *thurirl*

Student (human apprentice): *thurae*

We-of-the-shell: *ashkayth*

Stormshell: *kepeskashka*

A stormshell is the group of dragons you train with when you are apprenticed to a dragon.

POLITE PHRASES IN DRACONIC

Many thank-yous.
Throden velkais.

Talk not of it!
Thric ukris su myr! — *The standard "you're welcome"*

I would be eternally grateful.
Isk naev evlyra velkai.

My heart cries for you.
Ur carvx dax ihk wux. — *That's formal Draconic for "I'm sorry!"*

It is an honor to see so strong a dragon!
Myr vi orik ekess ocuir zyak versvesh orik darastrix!

Though it cripples me, I must go.
Arssix myr thurgix ur, Isk boros gethrisj.

USEFUL PHRASES IN DRACONIC

I want to learn magic.
Isk tuor ekess parvex arcaniss.

Where is the bathroom?
Vessyx vi rax gurgulax?

Help! My enchantment goes dangerously awry!
Farwelis! Ur levex gethrisjs korthys agox!

COMPLIMENTS IN DRACONIC

Please take my small gift!
Jaeiss clax ur kosj majiks!

Your strength and knowledge are legendary!
Wuxa versveshys vur othokenta hys sjahax!

Legend pales before your brilliance!
Sjahax lunyr ghoros wuxa orthokenta!

Writing with Dragons

The script of Draconic, the language of dragons, is composed mainly of uncomplicated straight or slightly curved lines, all of which are easy to produce using a talon. Dragons do not always scratch their writing on wood or stone, though. As dragons possess opposable thumbs, they are able to use writing implements large enough for dragon claws, and parchment large enough for dragon letters.

Young dragons practice their letters with both talon and stylus on large beds of wet clay in their lair. If the dragon wants to keep the writing, it needs only to harden the clay with fire. If it wishes to erase a mistake or does not wish to keep its writing, it needs only to use its tail to wipe the surface clean again.

Of course, a dragon can always change into human form and copy the writing onto parchment, as well.

A teacher is called a *maekrix*, or "leader," in Draconic.

Magic Lessons

Dragons are born with magical powers, but they still need help learning how best to channel their powers. A wyrmling must train for seven years to gain mastery over its magic. Those whose parents either cannot or will not train them must seek out a teacher to train them in the ways of dragon magic. The *maekrix* is often a dragon with exceptional magical skills. But some dragons will send their young to a magic academy to work with a dragon master, a young wizard with a strong connection with dragons.

More about those two options later in this book!

Like a human learning to draw, it can take a long time for the wyrmling to learn how to use its natural elemental magic as anything other than a blunt instrument. A hatchling has to learn exactly the right amount of power to channel, as well as the speed, direction, and intention they should wield it with. Dragons have to have a firm grasp on exactly how their magic works before they can try to use it for anything complicated. After a young dragon can control its magic, it can learn all the different ways it can combine the fire with its other talents.

Experiment with your breath! Try whistling. Now change the shape of your mouth. Try experimenting with the amount of air you blow. Move your tongue around. Try blowing from your belly as opposed to your throat. Now you have an idea as to how it feels for a dragon to experiment!

THE MÆKRIX

Dragons have a saying: "Once a maekrix, always a maekrix." Even after dragons are no longer apprenticed to their master, they still refer to their dragon master as maekrix, and the dragon master still refers to them as *thurae*. While dragons do not owe their allegiance to their maekrix after training has been completed, a dragon will not move against its maekrix unless it has no other choice.

That's "student" in Draconic.

Dragon Magic and You

For humans, there are two basic ways to learn dragon magic—apprenticing yourself to a wise wizard dragon or studying alongside your own dragon wyrmling at a school for dragon masters.

Become a Dragon Apprentice

A maekrix accepts apprentices in groups of three called stormshells, or *kepeskashka* as they are known in Draconic. Sometimes a stormshell has a human apprentice in addition to the three young dragons. Called a *kosjirl*, which is akin to "pet" in Draconic, the human learns alongside the dragons and is often jealously guarded by the dragons in the stormshell.

Learning from dragons—the very embodiments of magic themselves—is not easy. It takes a lot of research to find a good maekrix and even more to find one who is willing to accept a human apprentice. You'll also have to work hard to convince the maekrix that you are trustworthy and useful, as dragons release the secrets of dragon magic only to those who have worked hard to earn the right several times over. Once you find a maekrix who will accept you, you will live in the dragon's cavern.

They call each other ashkayth or "we-of-the-shell" in Draconic.

Who is considerably less durable than a dragon apprentice.

Become a Dragon Master

A dragon master is a dragon's best friend from the moment the dragon hatches into the world—and that's a big, but rewarding, responsibility. The only way for a human to become a dragon master is to become a student at Darastrix Academy for Young Dragons and Their Wizards.

This school for future dragon masters and their dragons guides you through the process of figuring out what kind of dragon you should bond with, what kind of dragon magic you should study, and ultimately, what specific dragon is best suited to you. Then, alongside other future dragon masters, you learn how to care for and hatch your egg, make a lifelong magical bond with your dragon, and teach your dragon how to best use its innate magic.

As well as help you learn some dragon magic of your own!

DRAGON APPRENTICE

It takes a special kind of person to apprentice to a dragon, and the path of the apprentice is as dangerous as it is thrilling. You are isolated from humans as you learn volatile secrets of dragon magic and compete against your stormshell's draconic rivals.

As most stormshells do not include humans, you will be able to slip by traps and magical barriers to dragonkind, helping to give your stormshell an edge in games. You can also use magical items that dragons cannot, and your fine dexterity and small hands can help, particularly in stormshells where the dragons have not yet learned how to take on human form.

Dragon apprentices must be brave, intelligent, perceptive, and most of all, hardworking. Their devotion to learning dragon magic must be absolute, for dragons are demanding, and sometimes forget that their apprentices are only humans.

One of the first things a dragon learns is how to take a human shape—which makes polishing treasure, exploring cities, and reading books much easier (and makes talking to humans involve a lot less screaming)!

SIGNS YOU SHOULD APPRENTICE TO A DRAGON

1. You can't stop talking about dragons.

2. You find the idea of flying exhilarating.

3. You've studied all you can find on dragons, including my other guides to dragonkind: *A Practical Guide to Dragons* and *A Practical Guide to Dragon Riding.*

4. Sometimes people look at you funny, and you realize you've slipped into Draconic. Again.

5. You can't stop dreaming about dragons.

6. Thunderstorms excite you.

7. You tend to hoard pretty things.

8. You tend to think of rampaging dragons as "misunderstood."

9. You've never really fit in with human society.

10. You can't stop thinking about dragons.

Why Apprentice to a Dragon?

Human sorcery is a pale shadow of dragon magic. Flying on wings of your own, breathing fire, casting spells instinctively and at will rather than after intensive nightly study, and moving with the superhuman speed and strength of dragonkind—these are things only dragon magic can teach you. Apprenticing to a dragon and learning how to cast magic like one means that after your apprenticeship, magic will be as natural to you as breathing.

Destined for Dragons

Anyone who thinks that living, playing, and fighting with dragons—even young ones—is easy should think twice before embarking on this line of study. However, the rewards are as great as the risk, and for one destined to learn from dragons, no other path will do.

Should I Apprentice to a Dragon?

Risks

1. May be mistakenly eaten by a dragon.
2. May be inadvertently sat on by a dragon.
3. May be accidentally injured in dangerous dragon training.
4. May be unintentionally roasted, frozen, or poisoned by snoring dragon.
5. May be forever obsessed with dragons. ⸺

Too late!

Benefits

1. Learning to fly!
2. My new teacher will be a _dragon._
3. I'll be able to breathe fire! ⸺ Or ice, or lightning, or poison, or . . .
4. More research on dragons to send home to Aunt Moonbeam!
5. Best kender wizard EVER.
6. Did I mention learning to fly?

To learn more about being a dragon rider, read *A Practical Guide to Dragon Riding!*

Kinds of Dragon Apprenticeships

Dragon magic is a broad subject, and there are many different areas in which you may choose to specialize. It is recommended that first-time students of dragon magic select one of the following three apprenticeships.

Dragon Descendant

Description: Descendants of dragons themselves, these apprentices learn to tap into the dragon within and channel raw magic without the use of human wizard materials, gestures, and magic words.

Requirements: Must have a draconic ancestor

Length of Study: Ten to thirteen years

Recommended Dragon Stormshells: Red, Gold, Brass

Ever feel a bit reptilian? You can only select this if you have draconic blood.

Dragonfire Adept *Student of Breath*

Description: The vast majority of apprentices become dragonfire adepts. These apprentices can sprout dragon wings to fly on their own, gain the elemental breath of their patron dragon, and aquire the enthralling majesty and secret knowledge of dragons.

Requirements: Must be willing to work hard

Length of Study: Five to seven years

Recommended Dragon Stormshells: Blue, Silver, White, Green

Hand of the Winged Masters

Description: Working as spies for the stormshell they are apprenticed with, these students practice stealth, hone their senses dragon sharp, and learn how to channel the elemental fury of their maekrix.

Requirements: Must be good at sneaking past people and monsters

Length of Study: Seven to ten years

Recommended Dragon Stormshells: Black, Copper, Bronze

Dragon Apprentice Duties

Even though you are human, you will be treated just like the dragon apprentices. You will do chores, play egg games, go to classes, and study alongside dragons like classmates.

Chores

An apprentice must do chores for their maekrix, giving their maekrix some of their time as well as their hoard in exchange for education. Common chores include scrubbing a dragon's hide, polishing a dragon's treasure, cleaning out a dragon's traps, fetching pigs for a dragon's dinner, relaying messages between the dragon and neighboring dragons, speaking as the voice of the dragon in the nearby towns, and organizing the dragon's library.

Human hands can get hide so much cleaner than dragon claws.

My least favorite chore is separating hoard scarabs from gold!

Sometimes old members of the dragon's stormshell.

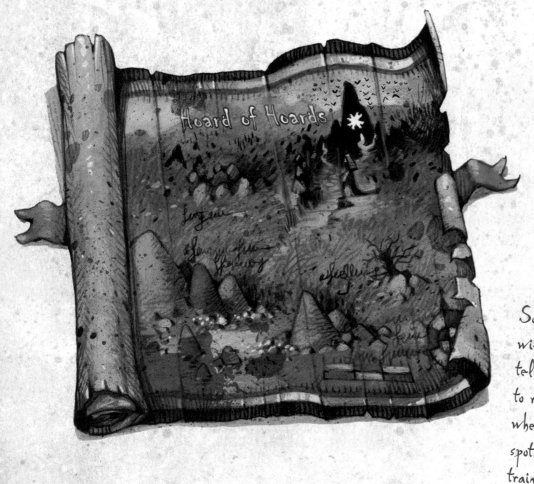

Hoard of Hoards

Sometimes, your maekrix will give you a map and tell you and your stormshell to retrieve the treasure where X marks the spot. This is very good training for the dragons and a lot of fun for you!

Learning

The majority of your time will be spent training with your maekrix and the rest of the stormshell. When you aren't actively learning, you will usually be given something to practice outside in the dragon's domain. Common assignments are channeling the element of air to fly as high as you can up into the trees, and collecting a leaf each time; channeling the element of fire to make a puddle boil; channeling the element of earth to raise small walls; and channeling the element of water to make stone turn to mud.

If you are not given an activity, you will likely be assigned research on ancient dragon magic. While this sounds dry, it is a great honor, as only those the dragon truly trusts are allowed in its library. Humans, provided they are fluent in Draconic as well as Common, are often chosen for this job, as their size and nimble fingers are more adept with books than dragon apprentices who have not yet learned how to take on the form of humans.

Stormshell Training

The first phase of an apprentice's training is very much like play. The maekrix will present various challenges that can be completed only by using magic. Then, as the apprentices work to overcome the obstacles, the maekrix watches closely to see what talents its apprentices display.

The second stage of training concentrates on the unique talents the apprentice displayed in the first part of their training. The maekrix will demonstrate a spell it thinks fits the apprentice's talents and then describes how it channeled its natural elemental magic to cast it. Then the apprentice will try to cast the same spell.

And most exciting!

The final phase pits the dragon students against other dragons in games and contests, figuring out innovative new ways to use their newfound dragon magic.

Apprentices often happen upon the beginnings of their new abilities spontaneously, but it takes study with a maekrix—who has seen a great variety of dragon magic and can describe the theory behind a given magical ability—to allow the apprentice's talents to fully flower.

Eventually the tasks get harder and harder, and the danger gets greater still, until the maekrix is satisfied that its students are expressing every ounce of magical talent they are likely to have and that they can perform well under pressure and in grave peril.

When you join a stormshell, you will be given a dragon horn, carved from a real dragon horn and enchanted so that if you blow it, the other members of your stormshell will hear you, no matter how far away you are.

Egg Games

The most challenging part of a dragon apprentice's training are the egg games. Egg games, played between two stormshells of similar level, are often used as a way to encourage young dragons to practice their developing magical abilities, as well as help them learn the value of teamwork. Young dragons, much like young humans, are much more likely to do something the less like work it appears.

Usually a maze

Capture the Egg

In Capture the Egg, each of the two stormshells gets a golden egg to hide in a single area selected jointly by the maekrixes of the two stormshells. The stormshells have one day to set up whatever traps, misdirection, or barriers they wish around the egg. The goal is to capture the opposing stormshell's egg and keep the other team from capturing your egg. There is no safe territory, and dragons are allowed to defend their eggs, making for an action-packed game that can last weeks.

Blind Dragon's Bluff

In Blind Dragon's Bluff, the dragons are all blindfolded, save for one dragon on each team, called the "Seer." Then, large bells are tied around the tails of the remaining dragons. The Seers' goal is to "see" for the rest of the dragons in their stormshell, and to help them claim all the bells off the opposing team while retaining all their own bells. The dragons are allowed to use whatever magic and misdirection comes to mind, but they cannot silence or remove the bells on their tails. The first team to gain all the opposing side's bells wins.

One young Seer tied a bunch of bells on tree branches in a forest to set a trap for the opposing stormshell!

What You'll Need

Here are a few items you'll want to make sure you bring to your apprenticeship among the dragons!

Dragon Rider Armor

No dragons were harmed in the making of this armor!

This armor is crafted from the cast-off scales of dragons rather than from dragon hide. That means it won't get you in trouble with any dragons you happen to meet. Specially crafted to aid you in dragon riding and naturally resistant against the type of energy the dragon who donated the scales wields, this armor is also enchanted to slow your fall should you ever take a tumble from a great height.

Invaluable, if you're going to spend a lot of time around dragons!

Goggles of Draconic Vision

Unlike humans, dragons can see perfectly in the dark. Also unlike humans, dragons have a number of ways to cloud the vision of mortals, usually by summoning magical fog or darkness. With these goggles, neither night nor magical fog and darkness shall obscure your vision—you'll be able to see just as well as a dragon!

Torque of Power Preservation

Not merely fashionable, this elegant dragon-magic imbued necklace makes it easier for you to use your innate powers! Think of all the extra practice you could get in when wearing this necklace. Hours extra a day, I imagine!

Ring of Dragon Friendship

When you wear this ring, dragons will find you charming, well spoken, and polite. In addition, they will also find that they cannot lift a claw to hurt you! I cannot stress how helpful this is when you're planning on spending time among the more . . . excitable of dragonkind.

Magic items have another use as well: if you ever need to bribe a dragon, feed it a magic item! The dragon gets some temporary magical abilities, and according to my dragon friends, magic tastes good!

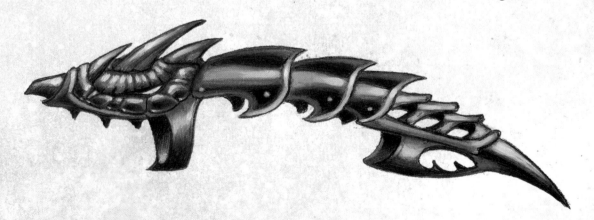

Where You'll Stay

As a dragon apprentice, you will live with your maekrix and your stormshell in the maekrix's caverns. Be sure to bring everything you think you might need to live comfortably, as unless you are staying with silver dragons, they are unlikely to have thought to provide human comforts. Their cavernous domains, however, often provide other advantages.

Bed, clothes, blankets, silverware, etc.

Ever made anything happen without meaning to? Ever have extraordinary luck? These are signs of being a sorcerer!

DRACONIC HERITAGE

During a thunderstorm, do you sometimes feel lightning racing through your veins, begging to be unleashed? When building a campfire, do you ever have to stop yourself from building it bigger–and higher–than strictly necessary? Do you ever see a herd of cattle and think, "Ooh! Lunch!"

If so, you might have some dragon blood yourself! Legend has it that all sorcerers– those magic-users who don't have to study spells, but who have innate magical ability–have some measure of dragon blood. Those with more than a measure are the ideal dragon apprentices. If you embrace your draconic heritage and embark on the study of dragon magic, you can learn to draw out the dragon within.

This is a map of the stormshell caverns I stayed in when I visited Faramyre the silver dragon and the Ornyx stormshell!

Underwater Entry

Observatory

Main Hall

Treasury

Conversation Room

Secret Door

Fresh Cistern

Kitchens

Guest Room

Supply Room

Guard Room

Library

Sleeping Chamber

Main Entrance

Secret Door

Secret Exit

The Dragon Pact

A dragon pact is an agreement you make with a maekrix, where the maekrix promises to teach you dragon magic in return for gifts or service. The magic of the agreement forges a lifelong bond between you and the dragon, just as living alongside the dragons and learning their ways will surely do. Anyone who wishes to learn magic at the foot of a maekrix must go through the following steps:

The Research

First, you must decide what kind of dragon you want to apprentice to. There are many factors to consider when choosing a dragon, the most important of which is what kind of magic you want to learn. Then, you should consider what kind of dragon you prefer. Study the habits and personalities of the different dragons who practice the kind of magic you like! Then talk to local wizards to find out which maekrixes have accepted human apprentices in the past.

For example, apprentices interested in fire magic should look into red, brass, and gold dragons.

See the chapter on dragon stormshells to select the right maekrix for you!

The Call

Find somewhere secluded, such as a library. Then, focus all your will on calling the dragon you want to attract. You will be able to tell that a dragon is interested when you hear its voice in your head. Arrange to meet the dragon to finish the bargain in person.

This stage is also sometimes known as "The Bargaining."

If the dragon refuses to meet you, you should probably find a different dragon!

The Gift

You must offer a dragon something of value to get it to partner with you. Usually this is a treasure for the dragon to add to its hoard, but some dragons require more—promises of service, lands, or whatever strikes the dragon's fancy. Make sure you don't promise anything you will regret—or can't deliver! Even the kindest of dragons will not forgive someone who breaks a bargain.

What do you get the dragon that has everything? Very powerful dragons sometimes require large gifts, but just as often, they have more use for entertainment and friendship than still more treasures and lands.

The Pledge

The pledge takes place at the dragon's lair and is part of the ceremony where you give your gift to the dragon and the dragon formally accepts you as an apprentice. Bow when you give your gift to the dragon, then recite the standard pledge.

If the dragon accepts you, it will call you *thurae*, the dragon word for apprentice. Then, both dragon and human recite their promises to the other, setting the terms of the magical contract. When both parties are satisfied, they seal the contract.

The Results

The moment you seal the pact with the dragon, the treasure you offered is immediately transferred to the dragon's hoard, and you are bound by magical contract to do whatever else you promised, usually with severe consequences should you fail.

The sealing of a dragon pact gives the dragon some of your magical potential and instills in you some of the dragon's magical abilities, such as breathing fire. Over time, you will become more like a dragon and less like a human in your casting of spells.

This magical contract is called a geas, and can be broken only by a wizard more powerful than the dragon who bound you.

The Pledge

Take this gift of magic and gold,
Teach me the ways of the dragons of old.

In return I'll lend you my hand,
Joining your efforts wherever they stand.

VALUABLE ALLIES, TERRIBLE ENEMIES

Be very careful about who you make your dragon pact with, for while it can be broken, breaking a vow to a dragon is never a smart thing to do. If you break your pact to a maekrix, not only will your former teacher come after you to teach you a lesson, so will the entire stormshell you apprenticed with. On the other hand, if you are ever in trouble and need aid, you can always count upon the dragons in your stormshell to help you.

Use your dragon horn to call them!

DRAGON STORMSHELLS

To aid in the very difficult task of picking a stormshell and a dragon to apprentice to, on the following pages you'll find a list of all the most prominent stormshells least likely to mistake you for dinner.

Are you leaning toward becoming a dragon apprentice? The only way to make this dream a reality is to find a maekrix to teach you.

For every kind of elemental dragon magic, there are at least two kinds of dragons who practice it—one chromatic, and one metallic, two sides of the same coin. Chromatic dragons embrace the destructive side of their innate abilities and use their magic for personal gain. Metallic dragons, on the other hand, see it as their responsibility to use their powers for the good of those around them.

While there are always exceptions among every variety of dragon, in general, if you choose a metallic dragon, you should be prepared to be held to a very high moral standard, whereas if you choose a chromatic dragon, you must be prepared to constantly strive against the chromatic dragon's darker instincts.

MOVING INTO A STORMSHELL

1. Do all the research you can on the type of dragon you will be spending time with. Otherwise, the dragons may mistake you for a talking, walking snack!

2. Bring gifts for all the members.

The biggest gift should be for the maekrix.

3. Bring only a small bag of your supplies. Leave everything but the bare necessities at home. You don't want to fill up the dragon's cave with human stuff.

4. Wear the same color clothing as the dragon you are living with.

Especially if it's a blue dragon. They love the color blue!

Chromatic Dragons

But totally fascinating!

Chromatic dragons embody the destructive and catastrophic side of nature. Selfish, ambitious, greedy, proud, cruel, and fickle, chromatic dragons are natural catastrophes—cataclysms for those unfortunate enough to encounter one. So if you want to learn powerful destruction magic, you'll want to make a bond with a chromatic dragon.

But how lucky to see a chromatic dragon in action!

To build a relationship with a chromatic dragon, you will need to be particularly persuasive. After all, from the dragon's perspective, it has already done you the favor of letting you live!

Living with Chromatic Dragons

Living with a chromatic dragon is risky at best—deadly at worst—but it is never boring. Be sure you word your agreement very carefully to ensure good treatment and solid education, and work your hardest to please your maekrix at all times.

You will also definitely want to procure a Ring of Dragon Friendship, which will prevent the dragons you are living with from attacking you if they are in a foul mood.

You can often appease a chromatic dragon with the gift of fresh meat like a snake or lizard!

Kinds of Chromatic Dragons

Chromatic dragons come in red, blue, black, green, and white.

Red

Blue

Reds and Blues are the most magically inclined, but proudest and difficult to convince.

Blacks and Greens are foul tempered and likely to attack you on sight, but are most likely to have use for nondragons.

Black

Green

White

Whites are the hardest to track down. They're not the proudest of dragons, but very independent. You will have to prove your worth doubly to them.

Red Dragon Stormshell: Charstryx

You can't show a moment's fear or hesitation if you want to find your way deep into the heart of the Deathshead Mountains, to where the red dragon stormshell Charstryx makes its lair. Led by the fearsome elder red dragon Loethar, the Charstryx stormshell is fast becoming the most respected stormshell in the world. Red dragons are usually kept in check by their pride, greed, and unwillingness to work together, but Loethar, with his strong belief in the rights of dragonkind, has united them the way no one else has been able to.

More like feared!

On which I received many a lecture!

REASONS TO LIVE WITH RED DRAGONS

1. Best roast marshmallows ever

2. Keep warm snuggled against their always-toasty scales

3. Unforgettable fire shows after dark

4. Awesome scavenger hunts

You'll learn how to do this by stomping your foot!

Red Dragon Magic

The Charstryx stormshell specializes in fire and earth magic. With a slap of their tails, they can make the earth tremble. With a glare they can make the earth give up the secrets of hidden pathways and lost treasures, and they can exhale a firestorm. Look closely at a Charstryx dragon, and you can see the fire in its eyes and flickering across its scales—an amazing sight that causes most creatures to stand rooted to the spot, unable to move, or, if able, to run in fear.

The Way to a Red Dragon's Heart

Doesn't matter what kind, so long as it's worth a lot.

You will want to make sure you bring plenty of valuables if you want to convince Loethar to add you to his stormshell. The best gift for him may be a gift that allows him to easily find other treasures.

Red dragons eat meat—the more tender, the better. They prefer to eat young female humans and elves when given the chance, so be on your toes!

Better bring your own food!

Black Dragon Stormshell: Vutharyx

If you make it past the stinging insects, the vine- and thorn-choked trees, and the putrid, watery walkways through the Marrowsinge Swamp, you may just be lucky enough to meet the stormshell Vutharyx. There, in a den accessible only through the water, the black dragon Wyvrex makes his home along with three moody and violent young black dragons. Wyvrex has earned a reputation among dragonkind for his ingenious lair defenses and traps. Humans who show stubbornness, ingenuity, and a lot of coins to the Vutharyx stormshell have a chance of being accepted—and even appreciated—by this sullen but effective stormshell.

Or unlucky!

Or offer to spread their fame like I do!

Black Dragon Magic

The Vutharyx stormshell channels the powers of the swamp. A harsh thought will summon a cloud of stinging, biting insects that serves better than armor against fleshy opponents. A sour look from a Vutharyx apprentice intimidates plants into strangling enemies, and a glower gathers the shadows around the apprentice into a cloud of inky darkness. In addition, the black dragons of Vutharyx can channel the burning acid that suffuses the core of their being into a spray of acid that will eat through metal and stone as fast as if they were paper. *Maybe that's why they're so bitter!*

The Way to a Black Dragon's Heart

The way into a black dragon's good graces is through coins, plain and simple. So be sure to go to your local bank and withdraw every last copper if you plan on trying to worm your way into a black dragon's sullen heart, for you'll surely need it!

Black dragons subsist largely on fish, but rare sea creatures—scallops, squid, and oysters—are a special delicacy for this inland dragon. Not a bad diet, if you're going to live with them!

Don't worry if the fish isn't fresh—black dragons have a stronger stomach than most mortals.

Imagine having a hive of bees at your command!

SIGNS A BLACK DRAGON IS ABOUT TO ATTACK

1. Black dragon sees you for the first time.

2. Black dragon looks happy.

3. Black dragon's throat puffs out in preparation to spray acid.

Blue Dragon Stormshell: Ulharyx

Mystery and danger await should you venture deep into the Mirrorage Desert where the blue dragons of the stormshell Ulharyx dwell. The ancient blue dragon Haravyri, known as "Stormbringer" by her enemies, is the master of the Ulharyx, a secretive stormshell with powers and methods not fully understood by any outside its ranks. The blue dragons have an appreciation—and many uses—for mortals who are crafty, talented, and can keep a secret.

Like me!

Some blue dragons live by the sea. I've heard the pounding surf calms them. It reminds them of their own affinity for thunderstorms.

Blue Dragon Magic

A blue dragon can deafen its enemies by barking out a thunderclap. And by coaxing a storm into carrying its words, it can throw its voice as far as the wind can carry it. The dragons of the Ulharyx stormshell are particularly proud, however, of how they channel a storm's greatest weapon—lightning. Not only can they send lightning bolts crackling from their lips, but they can also release just one flash of it, blinding their enemies.

When a blue dragon is very angry, you can see lightning dancing on its teeth!

The Way to a Blue Dragon's Heart

If there's one thing blue dragons love, it is themselves—but they are also very fond of things that remind them of themselves. Sapphires are their favorite treasure, though you won't find them turning down other blue-hued valuables either.

I hope you're not afraid of snakes, because they—along with lizards and other desert reptiles—make up the main part of a blue dragon's diet.

And yours, unless you bring your own food!

"Kissed by lightning," as the blue dragons say.

Haravyri has a soft spot for this recipe—it got me out of many a tight spot!

Blue Dragon's Favorite Snake Fry

One large desert snake
Handful of smoked salt
Handful of cracked black pepper

Skin and bone snake. Coat snake completely with smoked salt and cracked black pepper, rubbing them deep into the meat. Fry briefly with lightning breath until outside is crispy black, inside hot and tender.

Enjoy!

Green Dragon Stormshell: Achuryx

Only the most resourceful will make it through the overgrown, poisonous Ghostwood Forest to where the dragons of the stormshell Achuryx reside. Avaryx, the maekrix of the stormshell, assumed the mantle of leadership when he killed the old maekrix. While bad luck for the previous maekrix, this proved a turning point for Achuryx. Previously a bit of a joke, the green dragons of Achuryx have become a force to be reckoned with. Green dragons bear a grudging respect for those who are determined, capable, and insightful enough to survive long enough in their noxious homes to meet them.

> ### Warnings Against Joining Green Dragons
>
> 1. They eat elves, faeries, sprites, and probably humans too! *And kender!*
> 2. They live surrounded by poisonous plants.
> 3. They are temperamental and hard to please.

An unfortunately common occurrence among the green dragons

Green Dragon Magic

Few have magic as evil as the green dragons of the Achuryx stormshell. The dark whispers of these creatures cause plants to grow tall, thick, and poisonous. Their strong will and sinister whispers also command mortals: with a single glare, these dragons are able to convince a human to give up trying to escape, and with a word they can then send that same human running for his or her life. Perhaps most frightening of all, the dragons of the stormshell Achuryx have mastered their venomous nature and are able to release it in a single, invisible exhalation of lethal gas that poisons first the mind, and then the body.

The Way to a Green Dragon's Heart

Green dragons are perhaps the hardest dragons to bribe, not out of a lack of greed, but because what they crave most are trophies from past victories. This means that if you want to cozy up to a green dragon, you'll have to do a lot of research on the dragon in question, and then track down several artifacts from its past victories worthy of its attention. While less expensive than bribing other dragons, it is certainly time-consuming!

White Dragon Stormshell: Aussiryx

Better pack your warmest cloak, for the dragons of the white dragon stormshell Aussiryx live high in the Ice Rime Mountains, in a lair surrounded by a perpetual snowstorm. A relatively new stormshell, the three members of Aussiryx are led by the legendary white dragon Ravinsky. **Ravinsky** is known for his isolationist tendencies, his ability to move undetected within his realm, and his use of ice to craft complex traps. Only the truly hardy and brave stand a chance of making it through the white dragons' realm.

White Dragon Magic

The white dragons of the Aussiryx stormshell are born with the soul of winter. Summoning the unforgiving cold within, white dragons are able to spit a torrent of frost that freezes their opponents solid—just the way white dragons like their food. With training, white dragons can use that same frosty breath to create walls of ice or let it leak through their scales to coat them in an even more resilient, glittering glacial armor. A beat of their wings calls forth a bitter wind that buffets their enemies, and by letting just a little of the heat of their temper spill forth, they are able to turn their snowy breath into fog.

You'll use a fan.

Those who live with the white dragons often find that the weather reflects the dragons' moods!

The Way to a White Dragon's Heart

Diamonds, fine crystals, platinum—all valuables that sparkle like the snow of its homeland—hold a special place in the white dragon's heart. Be prepared to come to the dragon glistening with icy treasures to earn a place in its home. In the frozen tundra, white dragons have developed a taste for frozen food.

Sounds easy, right? Let's talk after you've had to use an axe and pick for hours to try to free some tasty, ice-encrusted morsel for your maekrix's pleasure!

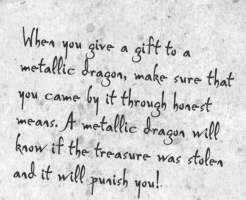

This would make a good gift for a gold dragon!

Metallic Dragons

Metallic dragons embrace all that is good and useful about the elements. Spontaneous and bright natured, majestic as mountains, and warm as fire, metallic dragons are nature's blessings on the world—miracles to those fortunate enough to meet them. So if you want to devote your life to learning, ridding the world of evil, and casting powerful defensive magic, you'll want to make a bond with a metallic dragon.

To build a relationship with a metallic dragon, you will need to hold yourself to a particularly strict code of honor. After all, from the dragon's perspective, it is doing you a favor, and you must prove that you are worthy by making a positive difference in the world.

When you give a gift to a metallic dragon, make sure that you came by it through honest means. A metallic dragon will know if the treasure was stolen and it will punish you!

Living with Metallic Dragons

Living with a metallic dragon is still risky, considering that you are living with a creature that could accidently snort a burst of deadly breath at any time. But aside from that, it really is a treat. Be sure you abide by every word of your agreement, work especially hard, and do nothing to draw the ire of the dragon whose stormshell you are in. Little is deadlier than the wrath of a metallic dragon that catches you doing something wrong while under its protection!

They hate the idea of enabling evildoing.

Kinds of Metallic Dragons

There are five kinds of metallic dragons: gold, silver, copper, bronze, and brass.

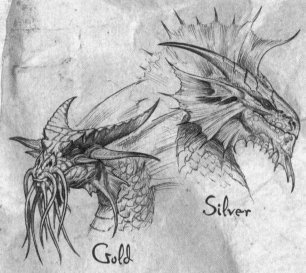

Silver

Gold

Gold and silver dragons are the most magical of the metallics, but also hold themselves and those they associate with to the highest standards. They may prove very difficult to convince.

Copper and brass dragons are talkative, playful, and easy to find. However, being somewhat less involved in society, they also have the least reason to partner with humans and kender.

Brass

Copper

Bronze dragons are very friendly, but hard to track down due to their love of the wilderness.

Bronze

Gold Dragon Stormshell: Auryx

Few prove strong enough of heart to earn a place among the gold dragon warriors of the stormshell Auryx. The gold dragons' home is found in the belly of a dormant volcano, where they can ascend to the heights to read the future in the stars, or descend into the comfortable warmth of the deep. Oroyalis, the leader of Auryx, holds a fierce belief in the good of his work. If you are committed to justice, love beautiful things, and are willing to work hard, you might just find a home among the gold dragons.

Which I heard much about during my stay!

Gold Dragon Magic

Gold dragons are infused with the brilliance of the sun. With a simple exhalation, gold dragons can breathe forth the fiery brilliance of stars. By keeping the inferno in their bellies and breathing air over that fire, gold dragons can exhale air so hot it drains, dehydrates, and weakens their foes. They are also able to see into the future by reading spots and flares in the sun and in the positions of the stars. In addition, the dragons of the stormshell Auryx have learned to draw back the veil on their brilliance, blinding all who dare to look upon them. *Can you imagine learning gold dragon magic?*

The Way to a Gold Dragon's Heart

Better become a good judge of art if you want to earn a place by a gold dragon's fire, for Golds are collectors of fine sculpture and priceless paintings. But that isn't the only reason pleasing a gold dragon is expensive. Gold dragons subsist entirely on pearls and other precious gemstones!

WAYS TO IMPRESS A GOLD DRAGON

1. Make a necklace for yourself and your dragon out of freshwater pearls and beads.

2. Write a poem for your dragon in Draconic.

3. Keep your lair super clean.

4. Be completely truthful at all times.

5. Learn the names and locations of all the constellations.

Gold dragons love a hard worker!

Copper Dragon Stormshell: Rachyx

In a towering, ancient rock cathedral within the Desertwing Mountains live the copper dragons of the stormshell Rachyx. The elder copper dragon who leads them, Pocyr, is renowned for both his heroic deeds and master craftsmanship. Pocyr is currently searching for his replacement among his current students. If you want to earn a place among the copper dragons, you had best brush up on your best jokes and keep on your toes because the copper dragons have a wit as sharp as their bite.

That could be you!

You'll want one of these on hand at all times when living with copper dragons, considering their diet!

VENOM ANTIDOTE POTION

Three tears from a nymph

One pinch dragon eggshell–crushed

One cup essence of willow bark

Mix first two ingredients to make a paste. Bring one cup essence of willow bark to a boil, then pour over paste, stirring briskly until the potion has turned sparkling gold. Wave your wand over the potion to draw a smile in the air, and say *"youet fawel kopelin."* Wait until the potion has cooled, then bottle it quickly to retain maximum potency.

Copper Dragon Magic

The copper dragons of stormshell Rachyx are masters of earth magic. They can raise walls of stone with a flap of their wings. By merely walking toward a section of earth and hissing their intentions, they can cause the soil to make way for them, and they can turn their skin to stone with a passing thought. And of course, copper dragons can exhale clouds of slow gas and streams of poison, both secrets of the deep earth that are the copper dragon's birthright.

You'll clap your hands!

And soon, yours!

The Way to a Copper Dragon's Heart

Copper dragons love the treasures that can be found in earth and stone. Rare metals, precious gems, statues carved from marble as well as valuable minerals, and even fine ceramics made from clay all are good ways into a copper dragon's good graces.

Be sure to bring thick gloves and venom antidote.

Catching a copper dragon's lunch is no mean feat—these dragons enjoy snacking on strictly venomous creatures! Scorpions, cobras, deadly spiders—if it can kill with a bite or sting, the copper dragon will be salivating.

Just make sure you don't get bitten in the process. That will really ruin a copper dragon's appetite.

Brass Dragon Stormshell: Bensvelkyx

Buried beneath the sands of the Goldust Desert is an underground cavern the size of a small city. Therein dwells the stormshell Bensvelkyx, living side by side with snakes, lizards, large-eared foxes, big-eyed mice, and other desert creatures. Jaarvyx, the leader of the stormshell Bensvelkyx, is devoted to the delicate balance of his homeland and considers his stormshell the guardian of the environment. If you think nothing is more beautiful than nature and can talk all night about any topic under the sun, you might want to consider studying with the brass dragons!

Brass Dragon Magic

Nature's favored creatures, brass dragons are imbued with the wind and fire of creation rather than of destruction. The weather itself reflects their mood. With a simple hiss, a brass dragon can cause a gust of wind or a gentle breeze, and by whispering a lullaby on that breeze, a Brass can send anyone it wishes into the deepest slumber. Their most well-known ability is to exhale a long stream of flame fierce as any of the red dragons know.

The Way to a Brass Dragon's Heart

Brass dragons are perhaps the easiest and least expensive of all dragons to please. Creatures of nature, brass dragons enjoy items made from plants: a rare cut of wood, a finely woven garment made out of cotton, and a pixie's best flower petal skirt all are worth more than silver to a brass dragon.

Keeping food on a brass dragon's table is likewise easy, if specific. Collecting dew drops in crystal vials at morning's first light is likely to be one of your first tasks as a member of this stormshell.

Brass dragons must be magical to subsist on so little, being so big!

A COMMON MYTH ABOUT BRASS DRAGONS

MYTH: Brass dragons are silly weaklings.

TRUTH: Brass dragons are brave and fierce as any dragon. They avoid harming even the smallest animal out of respect for nature, not out of weakness. But that won't stop them from crushing any blue dragon dumb enough to harm even a single creature in Brass territory.

You've been talking to blue dragons, haven't you?

Bronze Dragon Stormshell: Aujiryx

Get ready for a journey into paradise! The sun is always shining and the sky is always sapphire blue on Auraveil, the tropical island where the bronze dragon stormshell Aujiryx dwells. Aujiryx's maekrix, Liiravre, is the last living member of her old stormshell, which long kept the sea dragons at bay. The bronze dragons of stormshell Aujiryx are determined to prove themselves worthy of the legacy handed down to them.

Who wouldn't want to live there?

Bronze Dragon Magic

Bronze dragons draw their magical powers from summer storms. By sounding a low, bellowing note, they can call in the fog off the ocean. And they can shape and move torrents of water by curling a claw. The bronze dragons of the stormshell Aujiryx have even mastered the art of conjuring food and water from thin air to suit any guest's tastes, be they alligator, elf, or dragon. Their breath is the essence of a storm itself, either striking out with tongues of lightning or repulsing their enemies with the unbridled rage of a storm. Due to their relatively solitary location, the dragons of the stormshell Aujiryx have also learned to detect the thoughts of other creatures, so rarely are they intruded upon.

In your case, a finger.

Even kender!

But not only for decoration. Bronze dragons will also eat pearls as a fine delicacy!

The Way to a Bronze Dragon's Heart

Get ready to dive to the bottom of the ocean for your dragon, because more than anything, bronze dragons appreciate pearls, coral, intricate shells, and other treasures of the deep. But bronze dragons are also practical: when no sea riches are to be found, they will also admit their fondness for gold.

Bronze dragons like the savory taste of justice, and so eat almost exclusively cruel creatures of the sea, their favorites being sharks.

Silver Dragon Stormshell: Ornyx

I hope you like heights because the silver dragons of the stormshell Ornyx live in aeries on the uppermost reaches of the Razorback Cliffs. Faramyre, the stormshell's maekrix, is nicknamed Daredevil for his seeming lack of fear when it comes to flying, diving from great heights, and confronting evil dragons. Prospective students of Ornyx must likewise be bold, adventurous, and prepared to give their all in order to have any hope of being accepted into this elite stormshell.

MAKE YOUR SILVER DRAGON A GIFT

1. Draw your silver dragon a picture of you two flying together.

2. Make a silver dragon out of clay.

3. Use fabric paint to make a silver dragon shirt—one for you and one for your dragon in human form.

Silver Dragon Magic

Wind and high altitudes sing in the veins of silver dragons. The very breezes anticipate the silver dragon's will and can help the silver dragon fly faster and turn quicker or buffet its enemies out of the air like toys. Of course, all silver dragons can breathe out the high mountain wind with such speed and force that it freezes, either paralyzing its opponents with a coating of ice or battering them with the fury of a winter storm.

Red dragons call the Silvers airheads.

The Way to a Silver Dragon's Heart

Silver dragons are among the easiest of the dragons to please. Their love of travel and humankind leads them to prefer treasures that have cultural significance to remind them of the people and the places they've known. Jewelry, fine woven fabrics, and expert crafts are their favorites.

If you have a talent for making crafts, the silver dragons will be particularly fond of you!

Silver dragons are as adventurous at mealtime as they are in every aspect of their life. Every day, they have a different meal and different flavors, rarely repeating the same one twice in a decade unless it is a particular favorite. You might consider bringing your silver dragon rare herbs to spice up its culinary explorations and earn a place in its heart!

DRAGON MASTER

Dragon masters create a hush when they walk into town, a dragon wyrmling twined around their shoulders or padding along companionably, side by side, chatting. Most people are under the mistaken impression that the dragon is the dragon master's pet and engage in embarrassing behavior such as reaching down to pet the dragon's shiny scales and saying demeaning things in baby talk. Nothing could be further from the truth—or more insulting to the dragon.

Typically beginning at age eight, dragon masters attend a school dedicated to raising both dragon masters and their hatchlings, with both human and dragon teachers. Prospective dragon masters receive the letter inviting them to Darastrix Academy on their eighth birthday, after they've demonstrated signs that they would be good prospective students.

And dangerous!

One of my friend's dragons, Karatryx, tried to roast one woman's fingers for calling her a "keeyooot widdle bay-bee dwagon!"

Though some start as late as fourteen!

SIGNS YOU SHOULD BE A DRAGON MASTER

1. You know everything there is to know about raising a dragon.
2. You've always wanted to ride a dragon.
3. You often feel like you identify more with dragons than humans.
4. You write your journals in Draconic.
5. Your notebooks are filled with drawings of dragons.
6. You find heights exhilarating.
7. You already bought polish, a buffing rag, and a scale pick.
8. You can tell the difference between a black hatchling and a green hatchling.
9. You've been caught studying dragons at more than one recess.
10. You've always wanted a dragon for a best friend.

Why Bond with a Dragon?

When dragon masters first start out, they are just like you and me. But they make a promise to a dragon that in exchange for its egg, they will make sure the hatchling is well cared for, always served fresh food, taught everything they know, and given a lot of room to explore the world and their innate magical talents.

When a wyrmling dragon bonds with a human, it creates a much stronger bond than those created between adult humans and adult dragons. In fact, the very strongest bonds are created between hatchlings and young humans around the age of thirteen. Growing up together, learning together, exploring magic together, the dragon and human quickly become inseparable.

Gods help the man, beast, or dragon who comes between a dragon and its human!

Raised with Dragons

Dragons in particular like this arrangement, as their hatchlings are practically guaranteed a good human match. A school with a very good reputation is likely to be entrusted with gold, red, silver, and blue eggs—otherwise very hard to come by due to the proud and noble nature of those particular dragons. Less prestigious schools are likely to have white, copper, black, brass, green, and bronze dragons.

Like Darastrix!

SHOULD I BOND WITH A HATCHLING?

BENEFITS

1. Growing up together with a dragon for a best friend!
2. Get to cast dragon magic spells with a real dragon!
3. Flying through the clouds on my dragon!
4. Get to teach dragons about kender, humans, etc.
5. Get to hang out with other dragon masters and their dragons.

RISKS

1. Make a mistake and risk unhappy dragon parents' rage.
2. Once bonded, I am responsible for the dragon for a lifetime.
3. What if my dragon and I don't like each other?
4. I may be unintentionally eaten by my dragon.
5. I may be unable to talk about anything other than dragons.

New book idea: A Practical Guide to Humans?

Wait—I do that already!

Darastrix Academy for Young Dragons and Their Wizards

Each wing of Darastrix Academy is decorated and kept in accordance with the desires of the dragons housed there. For example, the white dragon wing is kept at -26° at all times, its walls are white marble with veins of blue, and hard tundra covered with powdery snow make up the floors. The blue dragon wing, by contrast, is sweltering—as hot as the desert the blue dragons come from--with walls of sapphire blue and floors of sand that the dragons can burrow into at will. You can see why wizards make particularly good dragon masters—for who else would be able to keep the dragons so happy or make sure their hatching conditions were exactly right?

Be sure to bring plenty of warm clothes!

Here's the letter I recently received from Darastrix Academy! Should I accept?

Darastrix Academy
for Young Dragons and Their Wizards

Dear Sindri Suncatcher,

Your excellent study and dedication to anything dragon has caught our attention. As an outstanding prospective dragon master, you are cordially invited to come live at the Darastrix Academy for Young Dragons and Their Wizards, where you will continue your magical education as well as learn everything there is to know about dragons.

Assuming you do well in your classes, you will become a candidate for an egg, which you will then hatch at the school. Darastrix Academy will aid you and your dragon both in your continuing education until you both come of age.

Darastrix Academy for Young Dragons and Their Wizards is the premier school for those who show potential for dragon magic. Our facility is first class, with entire wings devoted to each variety of dragon, an extensive library, world-class flying arenas, and contacts throughout the dragon and wizarding worlds.

During your stay at D

Egg Chamber

Egg Chamber

Gold Dragon Wing

Copper Dragon Wing

Silver Dragon Wing

Egg Chamber

Egg Chamber

Bronze Dragon Wing

Brass Dragon Wing

Student Dorm

Egg Chamber

Egg-handling equipment

Classroom

Spell components

Mail Room

Entry Hall

Dragon Hall

Flying Dome

Grand Baths

Headmaster's Office

Library

Grooming supplies

Classroom

Egg Chamber

Student Dorm

Green Dragon Wing

Egg Chamber

White Dragon Wing

Blue Dragon Wing

Black Dragon Wing

Egg Chamber

Egg Chamber

Egg Chamber

Red Dragon Wing

Egg Chamber

Dragon Master Responsibilities

The dragon master's responsibilities for his or her charge starts the moment the dragon breaks free of its shell, and lasts a lifetime.

When the hatchlings exit their shells, they are already as smart as your average human, just begging to be filled with knowledge of the world. They are born with the knowledge that they are dragons, a dominant species. However, as their primary source of care, you are in a unique position to earn their respect and affection. You are also responsible for helping them explore their innate magical talents.

For more information on hatching, feeding, and caring for your baby dragon, see *A Practical Guide to Dragon Riding!*

Suggested Names

Gold Dragon
Luminia, Borealix, Aurex, Aethyr

Silver Dragon
Karaglen, Vorella, Viviex, Iskar

Brass Dragon
Poccri, Kethenda, Myrikar, Svyrgi

Copper Dragon
Snydel, Rhasvym, Vaerie, Rachyr

Bronze Dragon
Immersa, Irathos, Aujyre, Wysvyr

Black Dragon
Blight, Sjacha, Malsvyre, Thurkyr

Green Dragon
Blister, Machuak, Verthichar, Vyrvesh

White Dragon
Rime, Aussyre, Gixa, Dartax

Blue Dragon
Dazzle, Kespecco, Korthyre, Karryte

Red Dragon
Scorch, Charyre, Ixynne, Valenar

Never force a dragon to do anything it doesn't want to. You can try to convince them, but remember, your dragon is a dragon and is staying with you out of affection. You don't want to upset that dragon—who knows you so well—and make it an enemy.

Naming Your Dragon

Your first responsibility as a dragon master is to name your dragon. Be sure to pick a name that is regal and respectful—one that acknowledges the dragon's heritage and personality. If the dragon does not like the name you give it, it may choose not to bond with you.

Gifts

Dragons all love to collect treasure, and one of your responsibilities as a dragon master is to help them start their hoard. If you go on adventures, be sure to always offer your dragon first pick of the treasure you find. Not only is it polite, but showing such respect for your dragon's desires will make your dragon particularly fond of you. You should also give your dragon gifts to mark important events, such as its hatching day, and occasionally just to show your appreciation.

Often called a "seed hoard"

If a dragon becomes truly fond of you, it will begin to offer you gifts as well for your own seed hoard!

Caring for Your Dragon

Caring for your dragon means keeping it clean and well fed, and making sure it has a warm place to sleep at night. Most dragon masters and dragons find themselves happiest sleeping curled up together.

Or cold, if that's its preference!

While dragons can clean themselves, just like on a cat, there are some spots that are difficult to reach, and scrubbing your dragon's scales is an excellent way to bond. Use a sea sponge with strong soap, a bristle brush and pick for difficult spots, and a rag with armor polish to really make your dragon gleam! Dragons find the process of being bathed both pleasurable and addictive.

You can find supplies in the grooming supplies closet, and I think you'll find the Grand Baths make an ideal place to bathe your dragon!

If you listen closely, you may even hear your dragon purr!

Educating Your Dragon

Dragons are intelligent creatures, even having just hatched. At a school such as Darastrix Academy, you will be taking most of your classes together, learning side by side. In some classes, you will even be doing activities designed to help you and your dragon plumb the depths of its magic by exposing you both to a variety of challenges and unique situations. It shouldn't take much effort to coax your dragon into exploring its abilities—most dragons are just as excited as humans at the prospect of learning magic.

Dragons are excellent students and learn very quickly just through observation. The best thing you can do for your dragon outside the classroom is to take it with you everywhere. But be careful. Not everyone is open-minded about having dragons around—particularly librarians.

Education is the reason your dragon was entrusted to you in the first place, making this a very important part of raising your dragon.

This is also an great learning opportunity for you!

It gets much easier once your dragon can assume human form!

The Draconomicon is my favorite book in the Darastrix Academy Library—you and your dragon will be spending plenty of time with it.

DRAGON PHYSIOLOGY

Make a Dragon Bond

When it comes to selecting a dragon, you don't find a dragon—a dragon finds you. In most cases, dragons that have an egg they are looking to bond with a human call upon Darastrix Academy. The teachers at the school select candidates for that dragon's egg. Then, the young would-be dragon masters are brought to the dragons to see which is the best fit.

In some rare cases, dragons notice a particularly promising human child outside the Darastrix Academy system and approach them, usually in the guise of a human themselves, to gauge whether the child would make a good companion for their wyrmlings or not. In this case, the human is almost always immediately offered a place at Darastrix, not only on the merit of the dragon's opinions, but also for the well-being of the dragon they have been entrusted with.

One of the hardest tests you may have to do is to separate hoard scarabs like this from gold!

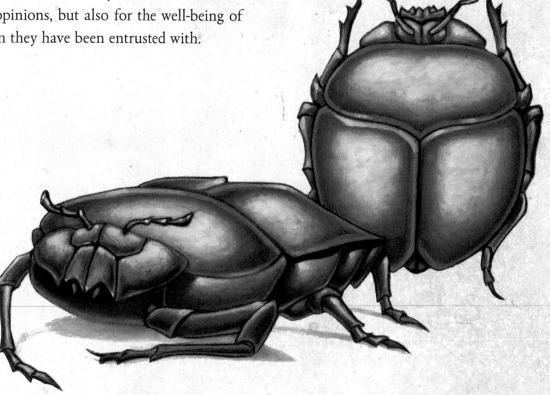

For dragons who value intelligence

To display physical prowess

COMMON TESTS

Riddles

Exhaustive questions about dragon lore or magic

Obstacle courses

Treasure hunts

Hypothetical moral dilemmas

Testing ingenuity and your ability to help start a treasure hoard for their young

The Test

Before a dragon will entrust you with its egg, you must prove yourself a worthy companion to the dragon's satisfaction. The form the test takes depends largely on the kind of dragon, as well as that dragon's individual personality. These tests can last anywhere from five minutes to five days, depending on how exacting the dragon parent is.

The Promise

This promise, made to an anxious dragon parent, is where you demonstrate that you know what a dragon requires and that you are up to the task of bonding with one and raising it. In your promise, you must display specific knowledge of that kind of dragon's feeding requirements, tastes in treasure, and educational needs.

The Egg

Assuming you pass the dragon's test and make a promise that meets the dragon's standards, the dragon will entrust you with its egg. This is where going to Darastrix Academy is particularly useful! The school has whole wings devoted to each kind of dragon, and within those, there are dedicated nurseries where young would-be dragon masters have all the resources they need to care for their eggs—and the instructions and oversight to make sure they do it right.

This is no small thing considering the exacting standards eggs require in order to hatch!

Dragon Magic

Helping a hatchling learn how to use magic is an educational experience for both dragon and dragon master. Few humans ever get to see how a dragon learns to channel their innate power, and the bond a dragon master shares with his or her dragon allows for an inside view to the whole process. Dragon masters use their unique perspectives as human wizards who understand the way dragons cast magic to meld the two into innovative and new forms of magic. If a dragon master shares a particularly strong bond with his or her dragon, the pair can even cast spells together that combine the best of the human and dragon forms of magic, going where no human or dragon could go before.

Finding Your Dragon: A Quiz

Find out what kind of dragon you have in your future! Are you going to study under the wise gold dragons? Or do you have a fiery young red dragon apprentice in your future? Answer the following questions and find out!

1. **When you have finally become a master of dragon magic, you will use your newfound powers for**

   a. The good of all.
   b. Personal gain.

2. **You have stumbled upon an ancient dragon's lair and woken the mighty beast. It is very angry, but also very bored, and offers you a sporting chance of leaving its domain alive. You prefer**

   a. To fight him.
   b. To challenge him to a battle of wits.

3. **A dragon in your stormshell has a beautiful, enchanted, human-sized sword in its hoard. The dragon will let you play with the sword once, and the weapon fits your hand perfectly. You can't think of anything you want more. You**

   a. Steal it or try to trick the dragon into giving it to you.
   b. Ask the dragon to sell it to you or demand it by way of force.

4. **You are a dragon knight, sworn to uphold the justice of dragonkind. You have finally tracked down a dragon outlaw, and it is holding a priceless work of art in front of it like a shield. You**

   a. Blast it with your dragon magic anyway. The dragon is obviously using it as a shield hoping you won't risk hurting the art to get to it!
   b. Try to save the art first—do you have any idea how much that's worth?—then fight the dragon.

5. **Two dragons in your stormshell are fighting, and it looks pretty vicious. One asks for your help. You**

   a. Force them to stop fighting long enough to answer some questions—such as, which one will pay you better, or why they are fighting!
   b. Leap into the fray!

6. **At Darastrix Academy, a dragon entrusts you with a golden egg as part of the test to see whether you would be a good dragon master for its egg. Unfortunately, you break it! You**

   a. Carefully construct a replacement egg or blame the breaking of the egg on someone else.
   b. Tell the dragon what happened even though it might mean failing the test.

7. **You come across one of the dragons in your stormshell crying. It asks you to help it get back at another dragon in your stormshell. You**

 a. Agree to help the dragon immediately.
 b. Talk to the other dragon first to find out its side of the story.

8. **A prospective student comes bearing a gift you know the maekrix will love. You**

 a. Take the gift by force or convince the student to give you the gift and present it to the maekrix as though you had bought it for them.
 b. Help the student find the maekrix and give him or her tips on presenting the gift.

9. **As the final segment in your dragon master test, to see if you are worthy of an egg, you are offered a choice: solve a riddle or complete an obstacle course. You**

 a. Choose the riddle.
 b. Choose the obstacle course.

10. **You are a dragon master, and your dragon offers you a gift of a beautiful set of silvery chain mail that is light as a feather and enchanted to turn away all but the sternest blows. At the same time, a dwarf comes by the academy asking if anyone has seen a set of enchanted chain mail that was stolen from it. You**

 a. Return the chain mail to the dwarf and apologize for your dragon.
 b. Keep the chain mail. It was a gift from your dragon, and besides, who is to say it's the same chain mail as was stolen from the dwarf?

11. **You are wandering when you come across two mortally wounded dragons, one gold and one red, collapsed on the ground. The gold dragon is unconscious, but the Red offers to teach you dragon magic if you help it—and threatens to eat you if you won't. You're down to your last healing potion. You**

 a. Give the red dragon the healing potion.
 b. Give the gold dragon the healing potion.

12. **Two stormshells are fighting over you! You**

 a. Watch to see which one wins or ask which one will give you more, and pick that one.
 b. Pick the one you like the best, or give them a test to determine which one you'll pick.

Answers If you received:

b, a, a, a, b, a, a, b, b, b, a, a: Better be on your toes, because your mischievous personality has you headed for the **black dragons**, who are unpredictable, sly, and relentlessly clever. Life is always interesting as the student or master of temperamental black dragons.

b, b, b, b, a, b, b, a, a, b, a, b: Alone in the wastes, surrounded by glittering treasure like desert princes, the proud **blue dragons** are difficult to find and once found, even more difficult to befriend. But once you have gained their trust, blue dragons make for fierce friends—whether they start as master or apprentice.

b, a, a, b, b, a, a, a, b, b, a, a: Have an appetite for leadership? Bold, demanding, and uncompromising, **green dragons** are hard masters bent on the relentless conquest of neighboring lands, but they are also very rewarding to the students or masters who please them.

b, b, a, b, a, a, b, a, a, b, a, a: I hope you like the heat because your fiery temperament has you headed for red dragon territory! Natural sorcerers, charismatic and proud, **red dragons** are among the wealthiest and most powerful dragons in the world, and make valuable familiars and teachers.

b, a, b, a, b, a, a, b, b, a, a, a: Better stock up on fur coats and snowshoes—you're headed for the frozen North where **white dragons** soar! Wild and untamed, the white dragons not only throw some of the best parties, they also boast unparalleled mastery of their homeland and make the coolest companions, be they master or apprentice.

a, b, b, a, a, b, b, b, a, a, b, a: Start practicing your Draconic because you're destined for time with the terribly talkative **brass dragons**! Brass dragons like nothing more than to engage in conversation all day and all night. In fact, you may need to remind them you need to sleep! As a student, you're sure to learn loads just from listening to these good-hearted dragons, and as a master, you'll never find a more eager apprentice.

a, a, b, a, b, a, a, b, b, a, b, b: Pack your hiking gear and get ready for an adventure because you're likely to be the future friend of a bronze dragon! Like the human rangers you are more familiar with, **bronze dragons**—with their use of dragon magic—are custodians of the wild, brave defenders of the animals, and curious explorers of the world.

a, b, a, b, a, a, b, a, a, b, b, b: I hope you have a good sense of humor because you'll be spending your days with the **copper dragons**. While not the most attentive of companions, life will never be boring among the mischievous copper dragons, and they will ensure you are as comfortable and entertained as possible—as long as you laugh at their jokes.

a, b, b, b, a, b, b, b, a, b, b, a: Be ready to work hard, for you have **gold dragons** awaiting you. Wise and devoted to justice, gold dragons are exacting but patient maekrixes, and demanding but rewarding students. Among the most powerful and noble of the dragons, gold dragons are the knights of the dragon realm, studying secrets other dragons can only dream of, and righting wrongs wherever they go.

a, a, a, a, a, a, b, b, b, a, b, b: Compassionate and devoted, **silver dragons** make the best of friends. As masters, silver dragons understand more about humans than we do ourselves, and often make exemplary teachers, explaining the mysteries of dragon magic more clearly than any other of dragonkind. As students, silver dragons are fond and intelligent pupils, as devoted to you as they are to their education.

Text by
Susan J. Morris

Edited by
Nina Hess

Cover art by
Emily Fiegenschuh

Interior art by
Daarken, Eric Deschamps, Vincent Dutrait, Wayne England, Jason A. Engle,
Emily Fiegenschuh, Tomas Giorello, Lars Grant-West, David Griffith,
Ralph Horsley, Jeremy Jarvis, Todd Lockwood, David Martin, Beth Trott,
Jim Nelson, William O'Connor, Anne Stokes, Franz Vohwinkel, Eva Widermann

Cartography by
Jason A. Engle

Art Direction by
Kate Irwin

Graphic Design by
Lisa Hanson

Visit our web site at **DungeonsandDragons.com**

A Practical Guide to Dragon Magic
©2010 Wizards of the Coast LLC.

Cataloging-in-Publication Data is on file with the Library of Congress
Printed in the U.S.A.
First Printing: September 2010
ISBN: 978-0-7869-5347-9
9 8 7 6 5 4 3 2 1

U.S., CANADA, ASIA, PACIFIC,
& LATIN AMERICA
Wizards of the Coast LLC
P.O. Box 707
Renton, WA 98057-0707
+1-800-324-6496

EUROPEAN HEADQUARTERS
Hasbro UK Ltd
Caswell Way
Newport, Gwent NP9 0YH
GREAT BRITAIN
Please keep this address for
your records.

620-25119000-001-EN

GET READY FOR ADVENTURES OF YOUR OWN

A PRACTICAL GUIDE TO **DRAGONS**

A PRACTICAL GUIDE TO **MONSTERS**

A PRACTICAL GUIDE TO **WIZARDRY**

A PRACTICAL GUIDE TO **DRAGON RIDING**

A PRACTICAL GUIDE TO **FAERIES**

A PRACTICAL GUIDE TO **VAMPIRES**

DUNGEONS & DRAGONS ROLEPLAYING GAME STARTER SET

KEEP READING UP ON MONSTERS, MAGIC, AND MORE.

Every book in the Practical Guide series is filled with exactly the kind of stuff you need to know when you're a hero.

Then grab some friends and go on adventures with the **Dungeons & Dragons®** *Roleplaying Game Starter Set*–it's got everything you need to start your career as a heroic adventurer.

DISCOVER THEM ALL AT YOUR FAVORITE BOOKSTORE.

  DungeonsandDragons.com